ARITHMETRICKS

ARITHMETRICKS

WORLD BOOK, INC.

CHICAGO LONDON SYDNEY TORONTO

World Book, Inc.
525 W. Monroe
Chicago, IL 60661
U.S.A.

Cover design: Design 5

ISBN: 0-7166-4100-3

For information on other World Book
products, call **1-800-255-1750, x2238.**

Printed in Mexico

1 2 3 4 5 99 98 97 96

Introduction

The puzzles in this book use numbers. But many of them are really jokes and tricks—arithmetricks!

You'll need a pencil and paper for most of these puzzles. And you'll have to know how to do addition, subtraction, and multiplication. But most of all, you must read carefully and use common sense. Many of these puzzles are easier than they seem, but they are tricky.

Some of the puzzles ask you to work out how many of something somebody started with. But all you are told is how many they finished with. To solve such puzzles you should work backwards. Take the last number the puzzle gives and start subtracting or adding as needed. In this way, you can work back to the starting number.

The stolen banana

A small monkey stole a banana from a big monkey and ran away with it. The small monkey ran 14 steps before the big monkey saw what had happened. Then the big monkey chased the small one. For every 10 steps the little monkey ran, the big monkey took 5 steps, but these 5 steps were equal to 12 of the little monkey's steps.

How many steps will the little monkey take before the big monkey catches up to it?

(ANSWER ON PAGE 28)

Careful, now!

1. Take a quick guess—how many is
   $10 \times 10 \times 10 \times 10 \times 10 \times 0$

2. Jackie walked downtown from her house in one hour and fifteen minutes. Coming home, she didn't walk any faster and didn't take any short cuts. But it took her only 75 minutes. How was this possible?

3. It had been a beautiful, sunny day. But that night, at midnight, a man bet his wife that it wouldn't be sunny in 72 hours. As it turned out, he was right. How did he know?

4. You're very sleepy, so you decide to go to bed at 8:30. But you don't want to sleep too late the next day, so you set your wind-up alarm clock for 9:00 in the morning. How many hours of sleep will you get?

(ANSWERS ON PAGE 28)

Three into twelve

There are twelve one-cent stamps in a dozen. How many three-cent stamps are in a dozen?

(ANSWER ON PAGE 28)

Two's from fifty

How many times can you subtract the number two from the number fifty?

(ANSWER ON PAGE 28)

The Rabbit family

Mr. and Mrs. Bixley Rabbit have six children who are boy rabbits. Each boy rabbit has two sisters. How many children are there in the Rabbit family?

(ANSWER ON PAGE 28)

Leftover sandwiches

Mrs. Martin made twenty-four sandwiches for a picnic.
All but seven were eaten. How many were left?

(ANSWER ON PAGE 28)

Even money

Two mothers and two daughters decided to go shopping.
They found that they had twenty-seven dollars, all in
one-dollar bills. They divided up the money evenly,
without making any of the dollars into change, so
that they each had exactly the same amount. How
was this possible?

(ANSWER ON PAGE 29)

Nimble numbers

1. When you add 10 to 100, you get 110. When you multiply 100 by 10, you get 1,000—a lot more. But what number makes a larger number when you add it to 100 than when you multiply it by 100?

2. What three numbers make the same number when they are multiplied as when they are added?

3. How can you make three 1's equal 12?

   1 1 1

4. How can you make four 7's equal 78?

   7 7 7 7

5. How much is double one-half of three-quarters?

(ANSWERS ON PAGE 29)

A square triangle

The numbers 3, 6, and 10 are sometimes called triangular numbers. That's because, if you show them as balls, you can arrange each group of balls in the shape of a triangle:

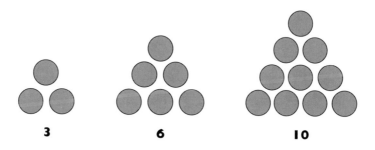

The numbers 4, 9, and 16 are sometimes called square numbers. That's because, if you show them as balls, the balls can be arranged in the shape of a square:

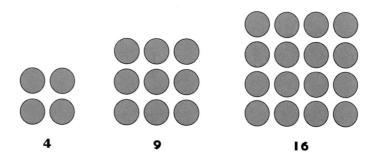

Many other numbers (past 2) can also be shown as either triangles or squares. But some numbers are both. What is the lowest number that can be shown as both a triangle and a square?

(ANSWER ON PAGE 29)

The explorers

Two explorers, a man and a woman, were making their way through a thick jungle. When they had to wade through a river, many of their food packages were spoiled. They divided the remaining packages into two equal shares and continued on their way.

By the time the explorers reached civilization, each one had eaten five food packages. The total number of packages left was the same number each explorer had started with.

How many food packages had the explorers divided?

(ANSWER ON PAGE 29)

The two hippos

There were once two hippos who lived in the same lake in Africa. One was afraid she was much too fat. The other thought she was too thin. One day, they decided to weigh themselves.

Their combined weight came to 8,100 pounds (3,645 kilograms). The fat hippo weighed exactly twice as much as the thin hippo. How much did each hippo weigh?

(ANSWERS ON PAGE 30)

The antique clocks

Mrs. Bedelia Gackenbammer owns two very old antique clocks. One clock doesn't work at all. The other runs, but it loses 75 seconds (a minute and a quarter) every half-hour.

If both clocks were set at twelve o'clock midnight on a Sunday, which one will show the right time most often during the next ten days?

(ANSWER ON PAGE 30)

The Klucksburg clock

The town clock of Klucksburg strikes each hour with a deep bong. Each bong lasts one second. The time between two bongs is one-fourth of a second. It takes the clock six seconds to strike five o'clock. How long does it take it to strike nine o'clock?

(ANSWER ON PAGE 30)

What time is it?

One hour ago, it was as long after one o'clock in the afternoon as it was before one o'clock in the morning. What time is it now?

(ANSWER ON PAGE 30)

Crossed hands

There are twelve hours and two minutes in the period of time from one minute before twelve at night to one minute after twelve noon. How many times will a clock's big hand move across the little hand during that time?

(ANSWER ON PAGE 30)

The divided watch

Lay two toothpicks across the face of this watch so as to divide it into three parts—and in such a way that the numbers in each part add up to 26.

(ANSWER ON PAGE 30)

The three robbers

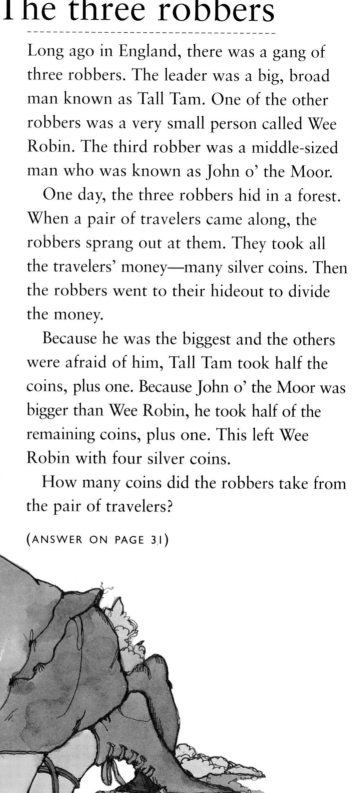

Long ago in England, there was a gang of three robbers. The leader was a big, broad man known as Tall Tam. One of the other robbers was a very small person called Wee Robin. The third robber was a middle-sized man who was known as John o' the Moor.

One day, the three robbers hid in a forest. When a pair of travelers came along, the robbers sprang out at them. They took all the travelers' money—many silver coins. Then the robbers went to their hideout to divide the money.

Because he was the biggest and the others were afraid of him, Tall Tam took half the coins, plus one. Because John o' the Moor was bigger than Wee Robin, he took half of the remaining coins, plus one. This left Wee Robin with four silver coins.

How many coins did the robbers take from the pair of travelers?

(ANSWER ON PAGE 31)

Generous Nancy

Nancy had seven cookies. She was a generous person, so she gave half of what she had, plus half a cookie, to her baby sister. Then she gave half of what was left, plus half a cookie, to her little brother. She kept half of what was left, plus half a cookie, for herself.

How many cookies did each person get?

(ANSWER ON PAGE 31)

Susan's grandma

Susan is a third as old as her mother, who is five years younger than Susan's father. Susan's grandmother is twice as old as Susan's father. Susan is ten. How old is her grandmother?

(ANSWER ON PAGE 31)

The bottle game

A girl went to a carnival. She saw a booth where people were throwing balls at bottles. Six bottles were lined up in a row. There was a number on each bottle. For twenty-five cents the girl could throw three balls. If she knocked down three bottles whose numbers totaled exactly 50, she could win a bicycle!

The numbers on the bottles were

15   13   9   19   12   18

Which three bottles does the girl need to knock down to make a score of exactly 50?

(ANSWER ON PAGE 31)

20

WIN A BICYCLE
SCORE 50 POINTS

Upside-down years

The year 1961 was special in a rather odd way. The number 1961 reads the same way upside down as it does right side up. And, more than a hundred years ago, there was another upside-down year—1881.

See if you can figure out what the next upside-down year will be. Remember, it has to look exactly the same upside down as it does right side up.

(ANSWER ON PAGE 31)

The Dobbs children

The Dobbs children were all out playing in their backyard. All their pet dogs and cats were in the yard with them. When Mr. Dobbs looked out of the window, he saw, counting children, dogs, and cats, seven heads and twenty-two legs. How many children were playing in the yard?

(ANSWER ON PAGE 31)

Growing younger?

Ellen's father is now five times older than she is. But he told her that in five more years, he'll only be three times as old as she'll be then. Is this possible? (You'll have to do a little arithmetic to find out.)

(ANSWER ON PAGE 32)

Black and white kittens

Marilyn's cat has had a litter of kittens. Some are all black and some are all white. Each black kitten has the same number of white brothers and sisters as black ones. But each white kitten has twice as many black brothers and sisters as white ones. How many kittens are in the litter?

(ANSWER ON PAGE 32)

The new kids

A new family had moved into the neighborhood. When Mrs. Frisby, a neighbor, passed the house, she saw four children playing in the yard. She could tell they were brothers and sisters, for they all looked very much alike.

"What a nice, big family," she exclaimed. "What are your names and ages?"

"I'm Carl," said a boy. He pointed to a girl who stood beside him. "This is Jennifer. I'm a year older than she is."

"I'm George," said another boy, "I'm a year younger than my sister Susie."

"I'll be eight next month," announced Jennifer. "I'm three years younger than Susie."

How old was each child?

(ANSWER ON PAGE 32)

Fishy stories

1. A girl carrying a fishing pole and a large fish she had just caught was walking by a lake. She met a man coming the other way.

   "Say, that's a whopper," said the man, pointing at the fish. "Have you had it weighed?"

   "Yep," said the girl. "It weighs ten pounds (4.5 kilograms) plus half its weight."

   How much did the fish weigh?

2. As the girl walked on, she met another man.

   "That's a good-sized fish," said the man, "How long is it?"

   "Well," said the girl, "the head is four inches (10 centimeters). The tail is as long as the head plus half the length of the body. And the body is exactly as long as the head and tail together."

   How long was the fish?

(ANSWERS ON PAGE 32)

Sharp Ears and Striped Tail

Two raccoons, named Sharp Ears and Striped Tail, had
gathered two hundred ears of ripe corn. Before they
could store it away for the winter, they had to peel the
leaves off each ear, which is called shucking. Sharp Ears
could shuck thirty ears of corn in an hour. Striped Tail
could shuck twenty ears in an hour. How long did it
take them to shuck all two hundred ears of corn?

(ANSWER ON PAGE 32)

Answers

The stolen banana (PAGE 6)

The little monkey will be caught by its eighty-fourth step.

The little monkey starts out 14 steps ahead. Then the big monkey starts to chase it. As the little monkey runs 10 steps, the big monkey runs 5 steps that are equal to 12 of the little monkey's steps. So, at this point, the little monkey has run 24 steps and the big monkey is 12 steps behind.

From then on, for each 10 steps the little monkey takes, the big monkey gains two steps. When the small monkey has run 34 steps, the big one is 10 steps behind. At 44 steps for the small monkey, the big one is 8 behind. When the little monkey has run 74 steps, the big one is only two behind. The big monkey will catch the little one after it has taken ten more steps.

Careful, now! (PAGE 7)

1. Any number, or group of numbers, multiplied by 0 equals 0.
2. It took Jackie the same amount of time both going and coming. One hour and fifteen minutes is 75 minutes.
3. The man knew it wouldn't be sunny in 72 hours because 72 hours from midnight is midnight three days later—and, of course, there's no sun at midnight.
4. If you fall asleep right at 8:30, you'll get only half an hour of sleep. The alarm will ring at 9:00, one half-hour later.

Three into twelve (PAGE 8)

There are twelve three-cent stamps in a dozen, just as there are twelve one-cent stamps in a dozen. A dozen is twelve of anything.

Two's from fifty (PAGE 8)

You can subtract two from fifty only once. After that, the fifty is forty-eight.

The Rabbit family (PAGE 8)

There are eight children in the Rabbit family—six boy rabbits and two girl rabbits. Each boy rabbit has two sisters, but they're the same two.

Leftover sandwiches (PAGE 9)

If all but seven sandwiches were eaten, then seven sandwiches were left, of course.

Even money (PAGE 9)

The two mothers and two daughters were actually only three people—Sue, her mother, and her grandmother. Sue was her mother's daughter, of course, and her mother was the grandmother's daughter— that's two daughters. Sue's mother was one mother, and her mother, the grandmother, was the other mother. Thus, they divided the twenty-seven dollars three ways, each taking nine dollars.

Nimble numbers (PAGE 10)

1. The number 1. When you multiply 100 by 1, you get 100. But when you add 1 to 100, you get 101.
2. The numbers 1, 2, and 3: $1 + 2 + 3 = 6$ and $1 \times 2 \times 3 = 6$.
3. Arrange the three 1's this way: $11 + 1 = 12$.
4. Arrange the four 7's this way: $77 + 7/7 = 78$.
   (7/7—seven-sevenths—is equal to 1.)
5. Double one-half of three-quarters is three-quarters. Twice one-half of any number is the whole number.

A square triangle (PAGE 11)

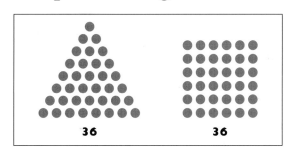

The explorers (PAGE 12)

The explorers divided the remaining food packages equally. In other words, each explorer had half the packages.

When they got to civilization, the number of packages they had left equaled the number each had started with. So, if each started with half the packages, the number left must equal half of the total they divided.

If half the packages were left, the explorers must have eaten the other half. We know they each ate five, which would be a total of ten, or half of what they started with. So, half of the total number must be ten. Therefore, they divided twenty packages.

The two hippos (PAGE 13)

The fat hippo weighs twice as much as the thin one. Thus, the thin hippo's weight must be one-third of the total, and the fat hippo's weight is two-thirds—twice as much. So, you can find each animal's weight by dividing the total weight by three. This will give you one-third of the total—the thin hippo's weight. Then, multiply that by two, and you have the fat hippo's weight.

The thin hippo weighed 2,700 pounds (1,215 kilograms) and the fat hippo weighed 5,400 pounds (2,430 kg).

The antique clocks (PAGE 14)

The clock that doesn't work will show the right time twenty times during the next ten days—at twelve noon and twelve midnight each day. The clock that runs, but loses time, won't show the right time at all during the next ten days!

The clock that runs loses 75 seconds every half-hour. This works out to one half-hour every twelve hours. Thus, at twelve noon on Monday, this clock will show eleven-thirty. At midnight Monday, it will show eleven o'clock. And each day after that, it gets farther off.

This clock actually won't show the right time for twelve days. It will have lost twelve hours in twelve days, so it will finally show twelve o'clock at midnight on the twelfth day.

The Klucksburg clock (PAGE 14)

It takes exactly eleven seconds for the clock to strike nine. There are nine one-second bongs. And, there are eight quarter-seconds, or a total of two seconds, between bongs.

What time is it? (PAGE 15)

If you think carefully about what this puzzle says, you'll see that one hour ago the clock showed just as many hours after one o'clock in the afternoon as before one o'clock in the morning.

Thus, one hour ago the time must have been exactly halfway between one in the afternoon and one in the morning. There are twelve hours between one in the afternoon and one in the morning. Half of that is six hours, which is seven o'clock at night. If it was seven o'clock one hour ago, the time now is eight o'clock.

Crossed hands (PAGE 15)

From one minute to twelve at night to one minute after twelve noon, a clock's hands will cross thirteen times.

The divided watch (PAGE 15)

Place the toothpicks as shown in the picture at the right. The numbers in each part total 26.

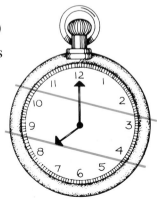

The three robbers (PAGE 17)

You can solve this puzzle by working backwards. The little robber had four coins. The middle robber took half, plus one, of the coins left after the leader took his share. Therefore, the little robber's four coins must be one coin less than the half the middle robber took. So the half the middle robber took has to be five.

This means the middle robber had ten coins to take from. Those coins were left after the leader took half, plus one, of the total coins. So, the ten coins are one coin less than half of the total amount. Thus, half the total must be eleven. Then the total number of coins the robbers stole was twenty-two.

The leader took eleven coins (half of twenty-two) plus one, or twelve. This left ten coins. The middle robber took half of those, plus one, or six. This left the little robber with four.

Generous Nancy (PAGE 18)

Nancy gave her baby sister half of the seven cookies, plus half a cookie. Half of seven is three and a half, and half a cookie makes four. So, the baby got four cookies, leaving Nancy three.

Nancy gave half of the three cookies, plus half a cookie, to her brother. Half of three is one and a half, plus a half makes two.

That leaves one cookie. Nancy kept half of what was left (half a cookie), plus half a cookie, so she got one cookie.

Susan's grandma (PAGE 19)

Susan is ten, so if she is a third as old as her mother, her mother is thirty ($10 \times 3 = 30$). Susan's mother is five years younger than Susan's father, so he is thirty-five. If Susan's grandmother is twice as old as Susan's father, then the grandmother is seventy years old.

The bottle game (PAGE 20)

She needs to knock down the bottles numbered 13, 19, and 18 to get a total of 50.

Upside-down years (PAGE 22)

There won't be another upside-down year for more than four thousand years—not until the year 6009!

The Dobbs children (PAGE 23)

Mr. Dobbs counted seven heads, so you know the number of dogs, cats, and children must add up to seven. And as the puzzle said there were dogs and cats, you know there must be at least two dogs and two cats. Four animals and three children would account for the seven heads Mr. Dobbs counted.

Two dogs and two cats, with four legs each, would account for sixteen legs ($4 \times 4 = 16$). Three children, with two legs each, accounts for six legs ($3 \times 2 = 6$). And $16 + 6 = 22$, the number of legs Mr. Dobbs counted. So there were three children playing in the backyard.

Growing younger?

(PAGE 23)

Pick any number for Ellen's age. Multiply it by five to get her father's age. Then add five to both numbers to see if one is now three times the other. It may take you several tries to find that if Ellen is five, her father has to be twenty-five, five times older. In five years, then, Ellen will be ten and her father will be thirty, or three times older.

Black and white kittens

(PAGE 25)

There are seven kittens in the litter—four black and three white. Each black kitten has three black and three white brothers and sisters. Each white kitten has two white and four black brothers and sisters.

The new kids

(PAGE 25)

Jennifer announced that she would be eight next month, which means she is now seven. So, if she's three years younger than Susie, Susie is ten. Carl said he was a year older than Jennifer, so he is eight. And George, who is a year younger than Susie, must be nine.

Fishy stories

(PAGE 26)

1. The fish weighed 20 pounds (9 kilograms). Half its weight is 10 pounds (4.5 kgs), plus half again makes 20.

2. The fish's head is 4 inches (10 centimeters). The tail is as long as the head—4 inches—plus half the length of the body. And the body is as long as the head and tail together.

    Therefore, to find the length of the body, we add the 4-inch head, and the 4 known inches of the tail. This is 8 inches (20 cm), which has to be half the length of the body. So, the body is 16 inches (40 cm) long. The tail is 4 inches plus half the body length (8 inches) or 12 inches (30 cm) in all. So, the fish was 32 inches (80 cm) long.

    Head: 4 inches (10 cm)
    Tail: 12 inches (30 cm)
    Body: 16 inches (40 cm)
    Total: 32 inches (80 cm)

Sharp Ears and Striped Tail (PAGE 27)

Sharp Ears could shuck thirty ears an hour and Striped Tail could do twenty. That's fifty ears an hour. So, it took them four hours to shuck all two hundred ears ($4 \times 50 = 200$).